red hat

by LITA JUDGE

Atheneum Books for Young Readers
New York · London · Toronto · Sydney · New Delhi

For Uma

ATHENEUM BOOKS FOR YOUNG READERS
An imprint of Simon & Schuster Children's Publishing Division
1230 Avenue of the Americas, New York, New York 10020

ATHENEUM BOOKS FOR YOUNG READERS is a registered trademark of Simon & Schuster, Inc.
Atheneum logo is a trademark of Simon & Schuster, Inc.
For information about special discounts for bulk purchases, please contact Simon & Schuster Special Sales
at 1-866-506-1949 or business@simonandschuster.com.
The Simon & Schuster Speakers Bureau can bring authors to your live event. For more information or to
book an event, contact the Simon & Schuster Speakers Bureau at 1-866-248-3049 or visit our website at
www.simonspeakers.com.
Book design by Ann Bobco.
The text for this book is set in Fairfield LH and Bodoni Oldface.
The illustrations for this book are rendered in pencil and watercolor.
Manufactured in China
1112 SCP
First Edition
10 9 8 7 6 5 4 3 2 1
Library of Congress Cataloging-in-Publication Data
Judge, Lita.
Red hat / Lita Judge. — 1st ed.
p. cm.
Summary: In this almost wordless picture book, a troupe of baby forest animals borrows a child's hat,
until all that is left is a long piece of red string.
ISBN 978-1-4424-4232-0 (hardcover)
ISBN 978-1-4424-4233-7 (eBook)
[1. Hats—Fiction. 2. Forest animals—Fiction. 3. Animals—Infancy—Fiction.] I. Title.
PZ7.J894Rd 2013
[E]—dc23   2012002600

Swish swash
swish swash

Fffwwup

Whoa

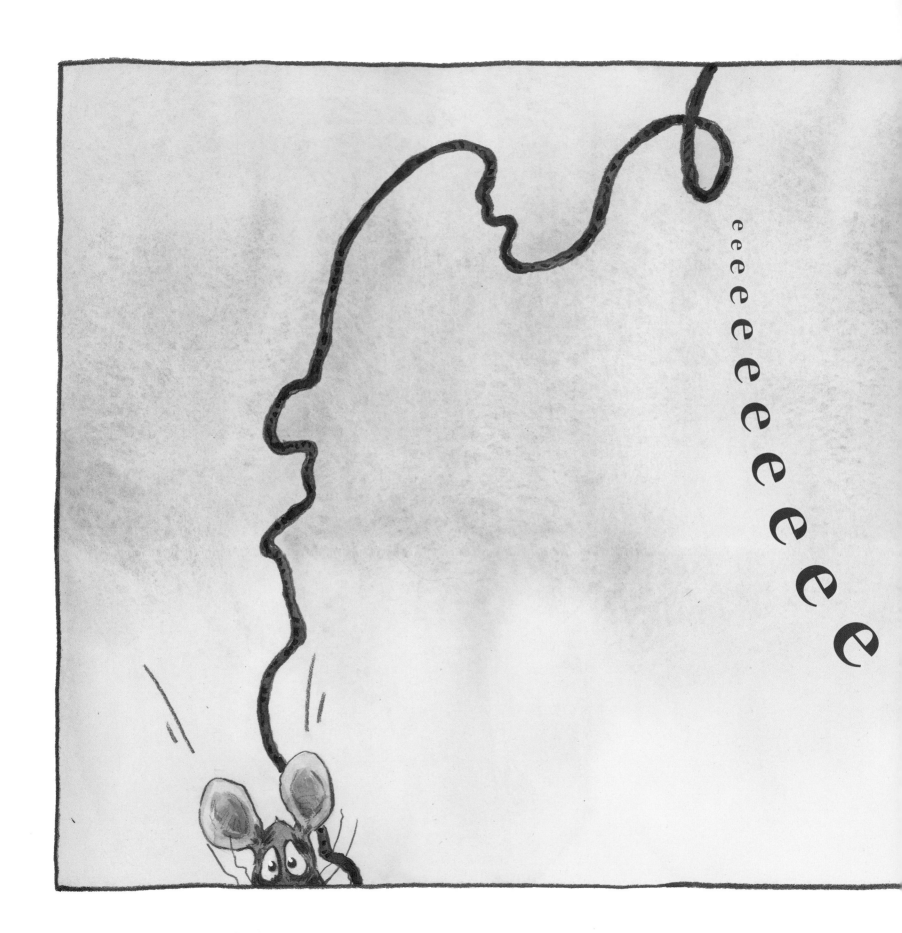

eep

Doot-do-doo

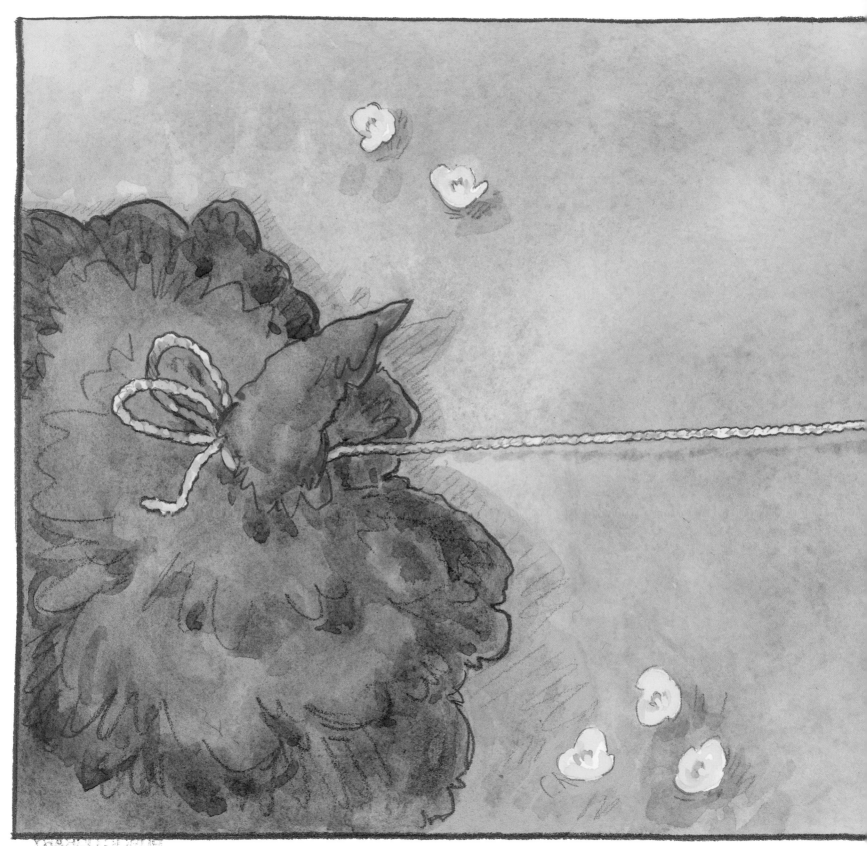

Tink-a-tink
tink

The End

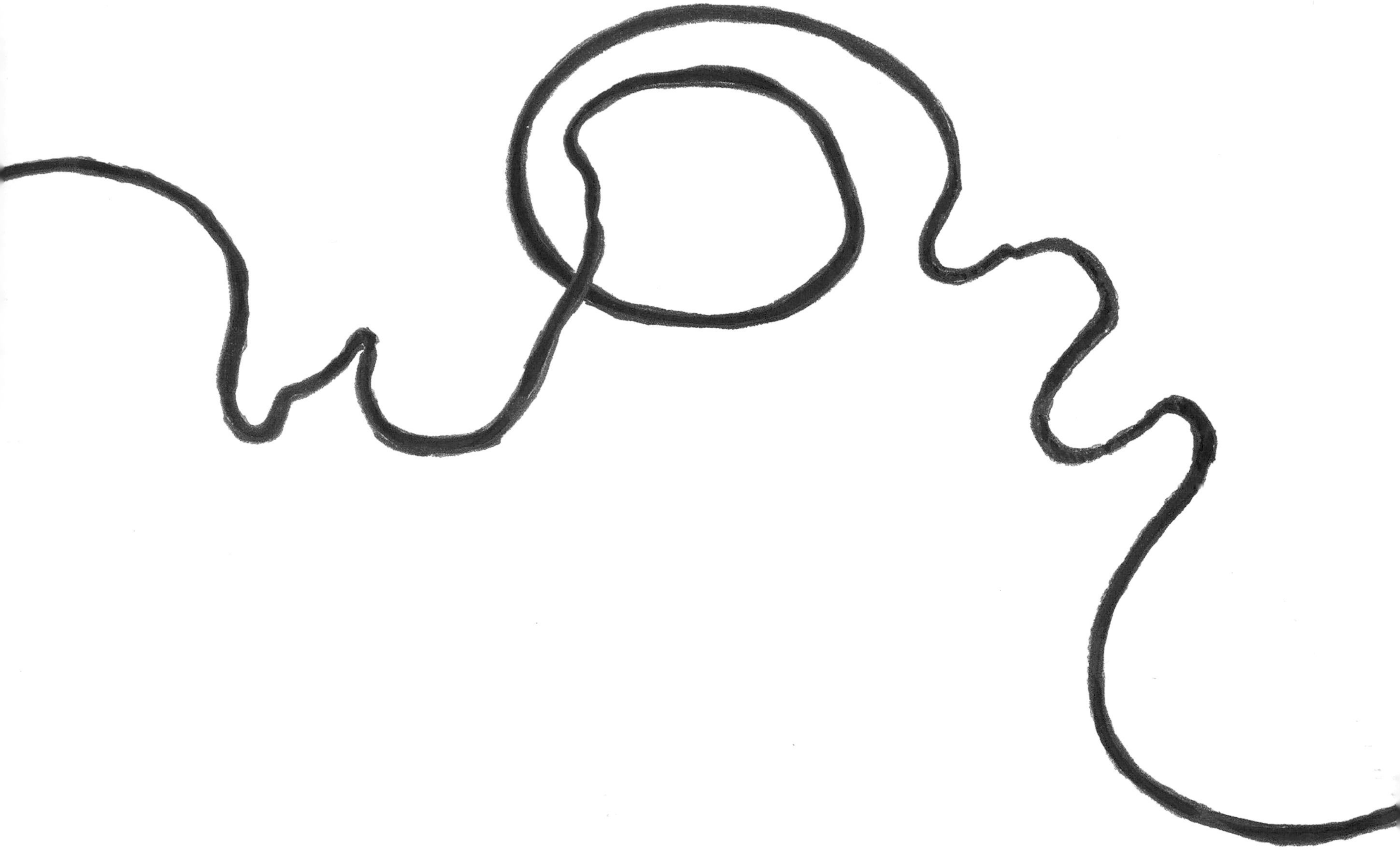